SHARING MY MIRACLES WITH YOU

Unexplained Spiritual Occurrences

By

Susan Marie Citro

Dedication

I would like to dedicate this book to my family and to my late husband, Louis.

I would like to extend thanks to my son Gary, who made it possible for me to complete this long awaited project.

On October 28, 1961, my family and I moved into our home in Mineola, L. I., New York. Our third son was born a week after we moved. We were always happy in our new home and when the boys were old enough I began to do volunteer work in Corpus Christi Church. I became a Confraternity teacher, and eventually a Eucharistic Minister in the church and for the homebound. We made many friends and were happy we moved there. A lot of our friends were from the church and we enjoyed sharing trips and different occasions with them. I also got involved in a prayer group with my good friends and found out eventually how much we gained being in this group. My husband became ill in 2004 and lived until April 16, 2012.

As far as the year 1996 and before that I have been receiving messages from Our Lord. My most memorable and treasurable message was received on June 6, 2008.

While entering Corpus Christi Church in Mineola, Long Island for Mass, I noticed that someone was sitting in the seat I usually occupied. It was a gentleman who I really didn't recognize but I decided to sit in front of him. Being a Eucharistic Minister I went up to the altar and started to distribute the Holy Host. I noticed this gentleman coming toward me. He appeared very pious.

After the Mass, I noticed him going up to the altar with outstretched arms in reverence. Not long after this I received this beautiful message from Our Lord:

My Daughter,

My Joseph was chosen by my Father to be the spouse of Our Holy Mother because of his spotless and beautiful character and his endurance in any situation. He, along with My mother, nurtured me in my growing years and offered me their utmost throughout those years, and he gave My Mother every bit of assistance, love, and accompaniment during the preparation of her role as Mother of Your Savior and the world. Every moment of those years was spent by him doing his utmost for her to fulfill her role as requested by Our Father. He will always be one of My most loved and cherished throughout eternity. After I rose into Heaven, I took him into Paradise and gave him his reward for his unselfish and complete submission to Our Father's will for him. My special gift to you was the appearance of My Joseph at Mass. He is always with you as I and My mother. Cherish all that we offer you, My daughter.
Your Savior

Another incident that coincides with this one is also an unbelievable appearance that I had at Corpus Christi Church. It was a Saturday morning quite a number of years ago. The weather was at its worst. We were having a blizzard, and it was so cold that the trees froze into icicles that really looked beautiful when the sun shone on them. I usually drove myself to Church but would not attempt it that day. My husband offered to drive me, and I gratefully accepted. After the Mass was over, I looked around me and noticed that none of the people I prayed the rosary with were there. I felt disappointed. After that, I heard a voice say to me, "Susan, do you want to pray the rosary?" I just shook my head "yes" but never turned around to see who it was because I guess I was not supposed to.

After we finished praying, I did turn around and saw this lady wearing a green velvet hat with gold trimming. It was not familiar attire during that era, but then I noticed she was gone in a very short while.

A few days after that, I was getting ready to prepare my next lesson for my Religious Education class. I was looking through my book and noticed that on one of the pages, there was a picture of a nun who had the same face as the woman in the Church. She was St. Theresa of Avila, Spain.

Sometime after that, my husband and I were fortunate enough to take a trip to Spain with Father Tomas Gomide. He took us to St. Theresa's Church, and her picture appeared all over the Church. It was the same woman that prayed the rosary with me at Church. We went on several beautiful trips with Father Tomas, where I experienced other incidents which will further appear.

Just a few weeks ago, I was reading a lovely little book given to me by a lady from St. Timothy's Church. It was written by Dolly Kimmes Cosgrove and was called "A Collection of My Favorite Prayers." In this book, there is a beautiful picture of St. Joseph and a prayer. There is also a notation by St. Theresa of Avila commenting about her great devotion to St. Joseph and how he never failed to grant her anything she asked him for. Ironically she asked him for me to be given the privilege of giving him communion. I still cannot believe it. I am in awe about this whole situation.

In 1994, Father Tomas planned a trip to The Holy Land, and my husband and I were delighted to accompany him with our friends. It was by far one of our favorite trips. While we were walking along the narrow way of the cross, I walked down a few steps, and at the bottom of the steps, a beautiful live red and yellow rose was waiting for me. Naturally, I picked it up and put it in a plastic bag I had in my purse. A few days after that, we were back at home.

Once a week, we prayed special prayers with our Sacred Heart prayer group.

After the prayer session was over and everyone left, I was inspired to get the rose and frame it. I put the rose on the table and went into the other room to put something away. When I returned, the rose in the frame was bleeding. It was an incredible sight and so hard to believe. I decided to take it to Father Tomas. Father explained that it was a special gift and that I should keep it in a special place at home. It should not be exposed because evil forces would follow it.

When my friend Miranda learned we were going to The Holy Land she requested that we bring her a candle from The Holy Sepulchre Church in Jerusalem. In the area of the church called The Crucifixion, a nun was stationed and we got two large candles from her. We lit one candle and placed it on the altar. I put the other candle in my purse. When we got back to our hotel, I opened my purse to get the candle and put it in a safe place until our return home. The candle was no longer in the purse. We decided to go back to the church which was nearby. When we got to the altar the candle we were looking for was lying flat next to the candle we had lit. Naturally it was quite a surprise for us but we got the message:

The candle should have been lit and remained there.

On Sundays, after Mass, I brought communion to those who could not attend Mass. While taking communion with this one gentleman, I would walk up the path leading to his front door and ring the bell. His storm door was made of glass, and while I was waiting for him to open the door, I would have a vision through the glass door of Jesus on his white horse behind me. No greater vision have I ever seen. These are beautiful incidences that cannot be explained or simply put into words.

I have always had a very strong devotion to St. Jude. On top of a closet in my home is a picture of Our Lord and St. Jude. One morning I went into that room and found a prayer to Our Lord and St. Jude on the floor. I made many copies of them and distributed them to several people. I recite the St. Jude prayer every day.

On the day President Kennedy was shot, I had a religion class. When the children came in, everyone was talking about the incident. I said to the children, "Let us pray to St. Jude for our president." When I started to pray, not a single word would come out. He was already dead.

One day at Mass, a woman named Lorraine came over to me and said she was interested in starting a novena to St. Jude. She had already spoken to our Pastor, who suggested her to speak to me. Lorraine and I began our novena on Wednesdays, and we prayed for many intentions. One day when I went to Church, one of my friends asked me if I had heard about Lorraine. She had a seizure and passed away. Lorraine was a beautiful person and was so devoted to St. Jude and Our Lord. She had given me a beautiful statue of St. Jude for my home, along with a plastic candle that didn't have any battery or means of being lit. After her death, the candle miraculously lit up for a whole week.

For over 25 years, my friends and I held a prayer group in my home called 'The Sacred Heart Prayer Group.' The prayers were given by the Lord, and several groups joined together every week. My special friends Marion, Lena, Minette, and Lucille came to our group religiously.

During the past two weeks, two of my friends, Lena and Minette, both passed away. They were both 98 years old. Through the years, we had several other members who passed away.

We usually had refreshments after praying. I stopped in to see my sister-in-law next door before we prayed. One day I planned on serving a pie, and I had forgotten to pick up the cool whip, which I wanted to serve with the pie. When I stopped in to see her, she handed me a package of cool whip. I don't even think she was aware of it. That was a hard one to figure out. I also got a beautiful message from Him about our prayer group.

Daughter,

Today is a very special day. Your group will gather and pray the special prayers I gave you.

These prayers are jewels whose value cannot be comprehended. In due time all your years of prayers will shine forth, and their value will glow like the brightest of diamonds. So much has been gained by these prayers that none of you will believe when you become aware of what you have accomplished for the world and yourself through this prayer group. The value has been stored away and has been gaining more and more graces as the years go by, and when the time is finally here for acknowledgment, you will feel my love, peace, and joy as never before. Thank Me for bringing you together to The Sacred Heart Prayer Group.
Your Savior

Before we moved into our home, we lived in an apartment that was in the portion of a house owned by my uncle. It was a house previously owned by The Otis Elevator family. The house needed some restoration. The ceiling in our bedroom needed to be refinished.

My uncle thought it would be best to do it when we left. We started to take down all the things that we didn't need and pack them. We always kept a crucifix on our bedroom wall, and I asked my husband to leave it up until it was time to move. The day before we moved, he decided to take down the crucifix. Very shortly after that, the ceiling fell. Luckily no one was in the room at the time the incident took place.

I have a series of prayers that I keep together and say every day. One day when I took my prayers out to pray, I found a prayer that originally did not belong to me.

A woman who lived next door to me had recently passed away. It was a prayer to Our Lady of Lourdes with her name on it. It appeared out of nowhere.

A close friend of mine, Mary, prayed the Rosary with me after Mass every day with a group of people. When she was 99 years old, she was sitting on her couch praying the Rosary. Her aide was with her. Ironically her aide noticed she became very quiet and realized she had passed away. One night I woke up in the early hours. I lay there quietly, and all of a sudden, Mary appeared by my bedside. She looked radiant and very happy. I blinked my eyes to grasp the reality, but then she wasn't there anymore.

She was gone.

In the year 1990, my friend Miranda who was born in Croatia told me she was going on a trip to Medjugorje, a town in Bosnia and Herzegovina. I mentioned it to my husband, and he said, "Why don't you go with her?"

Naturally, I said, "ok." It was a wonderful trip with so many experiences. I met this lovely woman Angie at the airport. We became close friends and roomed together in Medjugorje. Angie was a principal of a school for challenged children. Every night after dark, we climbed a hill and waited to hear from the visionaries about the appearance of Our Blessed Mother. While Angie sat on a rock, she turned on her audio machine to get whatever sounds she could of the event. While she was sitting there, this little child came and sat on her lap and started to sing in Croatian along with the visionaries. Angie was concerned about this young child being alone, and she questioned the situation. On the audio, you can hear her say, "Is this your child? Is this your bambino?" Everyone answered, "No."

The child remained there for about 40 minutes and then disappeared. When Angie got down from the mountain, she told the visionaries about her, and they said she was the Gospa as a child. That is how they referred to Our Lady.

Shortly after that, Angie called me and told me there would be a special Mass at Saint Aiden's Church in Westbury, New York. She asked me if I would like to go. I was very happy to go to Mass with her.

After the Mass, a very pious woman announced that she would be saying the Rosary and asked if I would like to join her. We agreed. I had never seen anyone pray the Rosary the way she did. She held the beads very piously and prayed so spiritually.

The next day while I was saying my prayers, I noticed this prayer card I had with the Blessed Mother holding the baby, whose face was the same as the woman saying the Rosary in Church. It was Our Blessed Mother praying the Rosary with us.

I spent four years in Florida with my sister. Unfortunately, she passed away on June 20, 2022, and my younger brother passed away the year before on August 5, 2021. It was very difficult to lose your loved ones, but the extraordinary experiences that I have had prove to me that Our Lord wants everyone to be with Him in eternity. We belong to Him, and He always tells us, "You are Mine."

For all those who find this hard to believe, I suggest you open your heart and mind to Him completely. So many people have learned who Jesus really is, and they can profess that those who put Him first in their lives live peacefully and joyfully knows that there is nothing He cannot do for them when they look to Him for aid.

A number of years ago, we went to Italy and The Vatican with Father Tomas. Upon leaving The Vatican, we passed vendors who were selling religious objects. We purchased two keychains of Pope John Paul 11. I placed one of them on my house keys. We took a trip to my son's home upstate in New York. When it was time to leave, I could not find my keys. My daughter-in-law told me she would search for them and mail them when found. When we arrived home, the medal of Pope John Paul was in the glass container where I usually kept the keys. My daughter-in-law called to tell us she found the keys under the bed, but the medal was not there. We already knew why.

While living in Florida, we went to Mass every Sunday at St. Mark The Evangelist in Summerfield. The altar had glass doors that you could see through. The chapel was behind those doors. Every week while looking through the doors, I would see people coming into the chapel and sitting in the pews. When I entered the chapel, it looked empty. I found out that I was seeing souls not visible to the naked eye attending Mass. It was an unbelievable experience.

Like most people with hearing aids, I have encountered many uncomfortable experiences with them. A few days ago, I misplaced one of the kits. I went through the whole apartment looking for it. I decided to go to the dining room and have my breakfast and come back later.

I resorted to much prayer before I returned to my room. When I opened the door to my apartment, the hearing aid was completely visible in the middle of the room on the floor. I know it was not there, and no one else was in the apartment while I was gone. My right ear is the problematic one, but for some reason, I hear singing and praying in that ear. When I am in Church, and songs are being sung, those same songs are coming out of that ear but from a different source. At times I hear beautiful music and also singing unexpectedly.

Here are some very beautiful messages from Our Lord:

My Child,

All around you are, seeking —what is going on? What can I do? Where can we go to bring situations to a complete recovery? The Earth, in its entirety, is struggling with its identity and with every aspect known to them. Turmoil exists in every capacity, in every situation. Questions are being brought forth to all those in advisory positions for answers, but lo and behold—-answers are far from their reach because they are in a complete dither and will try with all their might to offer an explanation, but the result is more confusion to them because the more they try, the more the complications engulf them. The answer to their dilemma is so simple. Seek My Father. Seek Me. Pray to My Mother. We have all the answers, always did, and always will. The hardest situation for us is just a prayer away. Much much more prayer is needed to absolve these calamities. Prayers that are directed to us. We control the Universe. My Father is seeking his humanity with loving arms, and I with Him. He is begging all to look to Him for answers, He so wants to help end the turmoil but needs their attention aimed directly at him wholly and completely.

Your Savior

May 13, 2017–100th Anniversary of Our Lady of Fatima

My Child,

This day, 100 years ago, opened doors to humanity. My mother took the children into her heart and introduced them to the world and its sadness and joys and showed them the glories awaiting humanity if they kept themselves focused on my Father and me.

The evil side of life was also shown, and the results and trials of those who followed that path. One most important request of Our Lady is the prayer of The Rosary. It is a treasure that has been forgotten by many, and many of the negative things going on in the world are a consequence. Prayer is our link to My Father. He hears and sees all and is aware of those who take the time to speak to Him and those who do not. Let yourselves not forget this very powerful tool. All humanity has trials here on Earth and must be aware that the recitation of The Rosary is the necessary link to My Holy Father, My mother, and I. To obtain permanent peace in the world, many rosaries are needed, and too many people have misplaced their beads. Look for them, find them, and use them. Recite at least one a day, along with the other prayers you offer Me.

Your Savior

My Daughter,

Keep yourself calm amidst all that surrounds you. You are being protected by us here. It is not easy to be serene these days of unrest and turmoil. Situations are so foul and unsteady but remember that the good surrounding you far surpasses anything else. Would you have reason to fear knowing this fact? '

Do you mistrust those that have your interest at heart? Would you believe that the negative force has more power than even I for an instant? Proclaim your faith in Me to the negative force. Profess that I am the One that you trust explicitly. Let it be known to all the Universe, the heavens, and to all that was ever created that I am your Savior, your Healer, your Great and Glorious Physician, Your Prince of Peace, Your Victim-High Priest, and the oh so many other names given to Me, the One and Only who gives you complete assurance, complete confidence, and complete hope forever.
Your Savior

My Daughter,

The days ahead will not be easy. Suffering is the only way I can fix the tremendous atrocities in the world today. Humanity has gone so far astray that it will take a monumental amount of help to get things back to their proper order. Every soul must be aware that they are needed to join together to assist Me in this endeavor. Your first responsibility is to be aware of what has gone astray. People's main concern is in a materialistic fashion. Electronics are ruling the world in every shape and form. Humanism is so far out of reach, which is causing tremendous turmoil. The confusion has reached a horrific level because of this.

You must take the time to accept the reality of who you are and remove yourselves from the course of mechanical gadgets. Look at each other and see the need that is there to recognize yourselves as humans. When you have accomplished this, you will find yourselves in a much more secure and peaceful atmosphere. And you will be able to listen to Me much more readily.

Your Savior

Today will bring back many sad memories for many people. The shock of this experience will remain forever in the hearts and minds of men. All those who gave their lives are reunited with Me and My Mother. They will never know sadness or pain again. Continue your prayers for your country, which will slowly be released from all turmoil and evil according to the effect of those who turn to Me for solace, peace, and who give up what they believe is the satisfaction of their desires. I am with you every moment, as is My Mother. Use your time to full advantage by seeking us first and asking for guidance. Nothing good happens without our intercession. Always bear that in mind and continue to address us in every situation, and we will offer you the utmost solution to your most pressing problems.

Your Savior

My Daughter

Continue your efforts with your friends in preparing and making beautiful beads. They will bring tremendous comfort to many, especially to those you pray for daily. Every rosary recited is a joy to My Father, Mother, and I. It gives us such happiness and elation while you are praying these beautiful prayers, and we cannot but join you and offer all that you ask if it is My Father's will. Too few people are familiar with these beads, and by your endeavors, they are reaching out to people and places who knew not even of their existence. They will bring wholeness and peace to many who use them in the way they were designed. Each rosary said is worth more than it can be comprehended now but will be explained and understood at the time when we are all united in The Father's Kingdom.

Your Savior

Daughter,

Any thoughts or words regarding My Creation needs much interpretation. Every human being created is one and the same regardless of race, religion, or creed. Every human being has an equal share in My Kingdom. From the beginning of time, hatred has seethed from the very depths of Hell and will remain until we are all one together with My Father.

Every person has their merits. No one should be judged by their outer appearance. All good was given to each individual when they came into the world, and the enemy forcefully integrated all feelings except love among us.

That is changing now and will continue to change through prayer groups, recitation of Rosaries, and of course, The Holy Mass.

Good deeds will bring my kingdom to its rightful place with Me and My Mother and all the angels and saints.
Your Savior

My Daughter,

Time is fleeting now, and we have begun My forty days in the wilderness in preparation for My journey to bring the world to its rightful place. No one except My Father and Mother knows the extreme sacrifice that was made by us to endure this ordeal. Many books have been written, many prayers have been said, many words have been spoken, but still, no one ever grasped the true encounter of this journey. The suffering still remains because of the cold hearts that still do not acknowledge the reason for that journey.

They remain oblivious to My journey, My suffering, and My death on the cross. But the day will come when they will be fully enlightened, and they will lament completely their lax attitude and their failure to recognize the reason for My cross and how much they have to gain by My suffering. Then all will rejoice at the outcome and forever celebrate with My Father and I and My Mother.
Your Savior

My Child,

You must not spend your moments worrying about unpleasant events in your life. Time is a wonderful healer. Spend your time enjoying My beautiful Universe.

Look at My sky filled with pure white in the midst of blue in the daytime and sparkling stars at night. The Universe is My gift to My loved ones to enjoy. Listen to the sounds of the firmament, the birds singing, and the sound of rain and weather patterns. Never dwell on situations you have no control over. Instead of those thoughts, put your mind and heart in My presence. Keep your thoughts in prayer, and in that way, only good will surround you, and a shield of protection will cover you. I am always with you. Remember that. I never leave. Your negative thoughts will let you feel as though I am not there. Not so, Not so. Remember these words, and together we will overcome all your anxieties. I love you, and I only want peace, love, and joy for you, My daughter.

Your Savior

My Daughter,

These coming elections are a prelude to My second coming.

Doubt not that I am returning to My loved ones and believe that it will be much sooner than anticipated. Pray with all your heart that My humanity will make the right choice for your new leader, and keep in mind that My Father determines when a child is conceived and when every human being has fulfilled His will on Earth and is ready for Heaven. No man knows when My Father is ready to remove him from this Earth. It can happen in the blink of an eye. Wake up, humanity, and look to your Father in Heaven for solutions to all your problems, insecurities, and fears. My Father appointed Me as your hope. Forget not that I live within every one of you and that My Mother is the intercessor.

Your Savior

The Shekinah (presence of God)

We added a back room to our home, which we enjoyed all days of Spring, Summer, and Fall.

One day I fell asleep on the couch there, and when I woke up, the whole room was filled with a light cloud-like appearance. I thought something was escaping from the basement, but the vision disappeared in seconds. The fact that my home was used for many prayer sessions and that the people involved were all very spiritual allowed this beautiful vision to appear.

When my son and daughter-in-law made plans for their wedding, a bridal shower was planned on a Sunday afternoon when everyone could attend. The day that was planned happened to fall on Pentecost. Many outdoor pictures were taken, and I had a statue of the Blessed Mother near a tree in the yard. When a picture that was taken of her was developed, a shekinah appeared above Our Lady's head. It was a beautiful view.

The White Rose

My husband suffered from lung cancer, and he went through chemotherapy and radiation for a number of months. Many prayers were being offered for him. One night during the very early hours I woke up from sleep and looked over at him. Above his head was a symbol of a white rose. It was very prominent and made me feel very uneasy because visions do not appear just like that normally. Many rosaries were being prayed for him and a white rose is a sign from Our Lady. I told many people about it and when he went for a checkup he was told that cancer was arrested.

Our Blessed Mother's Appearance In Pool

On August 15th, the anniversary of Our Lady's Assumption, my husband was in my son's swimming pool with my grandchildren. I decided to take a picture of them. When the picture was developed, Our Lady's image appeared in it. It is by far one of our most amazing possessions.

VISIONS

Whenever I was in the car at night, I would see visions of big buildings made of red brick with green shutters. I saw them on the corners of the streets that I was driving through.

When the car would reach the corners, there would be nothing there. The buildings were just visions. My estimation is that those are the kind of buildings we would live in, in the afterlife.

According to our Lord, we will not need food or anything, but we could still eat, and I'm sure we will still have entertainment and such.

I also see visions very often of outdoor auditoriums. Other visions are in the sky. Looking at the dark clouds, I see souls moving around. I believe those are the souls in purgatory.

THE BLESSED MOTHER, QUEEN OF THE UNIVERSE

Jesus always reminds us to go to His Mother for our needs. She will offer her prayers which are very powerful. Our Blessed Mother offered her whole life and existence to our Lord from before he was born, through all of His life and into eternity. He was her only child. When you read about His brothers and sisters in the Bible, it refers to all of humanity.

When Jesus was dying on the cross, He told John, "This is your mother." If there were other children, they would be there to care for our Blessed Mother. She suffered terribly along with Him when He was on the cross. Jesus always speaks of His Mother and wants us to honor and love her.